I hope that
find wisper.
& encourage.
Enjoy.

Windows of my Soul

The Words and Thoughts of Erica Nicole Hyneman

Windows of my Soul: The Words and Thoughts of
Erica Nicole Hyneman

Copyright © 2007 By Erica Nicole Hyneman

ISBN: 978-1-59916-349-9

All rights reserved. Printed in the United States of America. No part of this book may be used or reproduced in any manner whatsoever without written permission from the publisher.

Cover Design by McKinley "Rocket" Wiley

Published By Erica Nicole Hyneman
Cleveland, Ohio

EHyneman8@juno.com

Printed By 48Hrbooks.com

Acknowledgments

First and foremost I give all praises to the most high God for blessing me with the gift of poetry. Father God, thank you for your wonderful spirit. Without Him, nothing would be possible. I am so very blessed. To my family, the Hyneman family. I love and appreciate all of you more than words could ever express. Thank you for your love, prayers, and support in all my endeavors. Especially this one. To my all my "back in the day" family that was with me when I was a young emcee. Thank you for getting me started—you know who you are. Love and Respect to you all. I'll never forget where I came from. To every English teacher I've ever had. It's because of your challenges that I write today. To all my sisters of Camouflage Finesse. I love you all for who you are, as well as blessed to have you all as a part of my life. Thank you. To my big brothers in poetry, Chiefrocka Entertainment. I couldn't be more thankful for all of you. I still get misty when I think of my very first night at the venue. A world of thanks to each of you for all that you've done for me. Thank you to my Kamikaze and B-Side fam. Love ya much! To my sista girlfriends. Thank you for loving me and supporting me. You all are such strong, and beautiful women. Thank for being an awesome example. Thank you to all my friends who have supported me through this journey. I might not say it much, but I appreciate you more than you'd ever know. Much gratitude to all who assisted in this project. Your time and effort is most appreciated. Thank you for being a part of a goal, that actually became an accomplishment. God knew exactly what He was doing when He placed you all in my path. Last but not least, allow me to thank......YOU! Thank you for your love and support. God Bless....

Dedications

I dedicate this book to the most beautiful woman in the world, my Mother, Ms. Willa L. Hyneman. Thank you for speaking the gift of poetry into my life since adolescence when I didn't recognize it for myself. Your words were seeds sown onto fertile ground that has grown and flourished. An abundance of thanks to you. I love you always....

To my mentor, sister and friend, Ms. Nolana "Liberty" Price. Thank you for showing me the true meaning of God's love, and that angels on earth do exist. Thank you for being mine.

Words from the Author

I believe that poetry is in all things. It's in love, life, relationships, arguments, make-ups, break-ups, and everything else under the sun. I find it to be a great source of freedom. There are absolutely no rules to it. You make it your own. I write to exercise my creativity. I write for healing. I write to reach and teach. I write to inspire and encourage. I write to tell a story. I don't mind becoming transparent by sharing my life with you if it may help in any shape, form, or fashion. I want you to know that you are not alone. Writing is a excellent form of therapy, and one of the most simple you may ever find. Walk with me through a world of love, happiness, reality, imagery, expression, and experience. Journey with me through the Windows of my Soul......Take pleasure.

Peace and Blessings

Erica Nicole

Table of Contents

I. The Love Experience

Experience	8
Just Us	10
Admiration	12
Art	14
Soul Tie	15
One	16
Reflection	17
The Break-Up	20

II. The Life Experience

P.O.E.T.R.Y.	22
A Haiku or Two	24
ColorMind	26
Kingship	29
This Face	31
Dreamed of my Father	33
GOOD	36
Empty	38
No Tears	40
The Definition: Poetry II	42
A Haiku or Three or Four	45
SPEAK!	47

I.

The Love Experience

Experience

Drowning in a pool of memories that can fill mansions of you and me.
Though we never existed,
we did.
Jane and John Doe.
We float on intimate moments shared.
Shedding every layer of what the outside laid upon us, as we laid upon us.
You drenched in moisture of me, and I melted.
Became one with sweat beads and glands.
We glanced into each others eyes feeling we shared the same image.
This is therapy to our souls to fulfill outside voids, for it was only me and you that could do the things we do, or did like no other.
Smothered in intense gratification,
whispering our present experience and questioning why it's so good.
I wish another could perform the same to break my addiction of you.
With every encounter,
I was being sentenced to life with no parole.
A strong hold.
No escape.
Trapped into this very act time and time again.
Such a pleasant sin....a glutton.
Glutton to my flesh.
The best at it.

Never knew what sexy was until experiencing my whole body being kissed.
Not one spot missed.
You never caught the mist in my eyes.
Yes,
one tear to cry.
Symbolic of the beauty I felt.
The music we made.
Sweet rhythms played without an instrument in sight.
Just sounds of us.
Communication at it's best.

Just Us

In a crowded as well as smoke-filled room,
only we existed.
Many words encamped the air,
but it was only yours I heard.
Exchanged information on the interest of one another in subtle ways,
yet obvious through body language and eye contact.
Never touched you,
but felt every part of you and your entirety.
You flattered me.
Was new to me.
Felt magnificent to be in your company.
If given a chance to go to paradise,
I'd choose here instead...with you.
We keep it simple.
Idle chit-chat quickly became three hour conversations.
You'd talk.
I'd listen.
Although silence from me,
I responded in spirit and you loved it.
I loved you for it.
This beautiful stranger was dangerous,
and I became a risk taker in the blink of his eye,
and I didn't mind.
He constantly fed mine, and I didn't mind returning the favor.
So close felt as though the same blood ran through

our veins.
Even Helen Keller could see that we shared true intimacy.
Plus and minus metal plates laid upon our chest, causing us to never be apart.
All of this in one night.
Amazed to see how relationships have potential to begin so beautifully.
Just you and me.
Creating unforgettable memories only to last for eternity...

Admiration

You mesmerize me.
By the sound of your speech,
the size of your feet,
the brightness of your teeth.
I find you.
Sexy.
You intrigue me.
By the way that you think,
how I feel when we greet.
I view you...
Beautiful.
You inspire me.
By your creativity.
Your hard work ethic.
Your personality,
naked.
Transparent.
I admire you,
my rare and precious jewel.
You are the epitome of cool,
and I value you.
Look up to you.
Blessed to have met you.
Want to walk like you,
Talk like you.
I put you on a pedestal that some have never seen before,
and I adore you.
My thoughts of you are so far extreme,

for you mean the world to me.
I snap into reality to realize,
you'll never belong to me.
Just a dream...

Art

Mystic Reality.
Perfect Simplicity.
Inhale.
Exhale.
Breathe Deeply.
Lashes.
Closing.
Slowly.
Minds.
Free.
Digits...Palms... Explore.
Soft Skin.
Satin Garment.
Rhythm.
Harmonious Melody.
Light Wind.
Spirits Connect....

Memories...Last...Forever.

Soul Tie

I was wrong to let him in.
Opened my heart to him.
Gave him my all as if he belonged to me.
Loved the idea that he made me feel,
desired,
needed,
appreciated.
The sound of his voice was a great symphony to my ears.
My eyes were privileged to see him walk.
My soul was blessed to be in his presence.
To inhale his scent made for happy lungs.
His very being sent my emotions into overdrive.
This man fascinates me.
He is my poetry.
I've wished upon every star that he would belong to me.
Reply?
Request denied.
I tried to get him out of my mind,
but failed miserably due to a soul tie.
In acts of intimacy,
he gave me a part of him,
and he a part of me.
Can't shake it.
Everyday I awake,
I imagine you lying next to me.
The morning greets me with a cold, unoccupied pillow.
Fantasy turned reality...

One

Head cradled by large, strong hands.
He is man.
She is woman.
Kinetic energy between two,
makes for an undying unison.
Magnetic.
A Harry London mixed with Lyndt kind of love.
Souls pouring onto one another,
leaving no space for others to enter.
Kindred spirits locked.
Key swallowed into a sea of passion.

Never to be found again...

Reflection

Born an own individual.
My own person.
Never believed that there would be another like me.
Then came he,
beautiful he.
I looked into his eyes,
and seen a reflection of me.
He was just like me.
Just like me,
or morally like I.
Eyes like mine.
Skin like mine.
Never thought I'd see this day or time.
Time stood still at this very moment,
and our tongues are numb.
Overwhelmed by his masculine femininity, and my feminine masculinity.
Pretty.
Hues of blues, orange, yellows, and greens, I see he, me.
We.
Intertwine,
like the braids of a nubian princess.
Intertwine like nest that sits on top of tree branches, as we stare at one another.
Could I be his mother?

or he be my brother?
For our views looks as though we are from the same gene pool.
Swimming deep like wet ink on this paper.
Cooler than so what playing in the background by Miles and his Band.
Slowly enticing me.
I blinked my diamond shined eyes to see...
he,
me,
again.
We.
blend.
Like the seasonings of Mrs. Dash.
Blend like the wind in existence that make the days pass.
Blend like the essential nutrients in one glass of V8 splash.
Blend like the seasons of 4 out of 365 days,
amazing how our souls connect.
Bet, this is a dream.
Because I never believed that there would be another on this earth so perfect for me.
Quickly,
pinch me,
spin me,
360 degrees so I can see if this is real.
We stood still.
Touched we,
loved we.
No longer questioned this reality.
Beauty unseen.
Only through mine and his eyes only.
Lovely,
sent from above for me.

For we go together like white clouds and blue sky,
or lock and key,
for I am he,
and he,
is me...

The Break-Up

No longer do I imagine us,
but you and her instead.
Heart bled when I got the news.
Is this lie in my mind true?
Yes.
Results negative from blood test.
God Bless.
No stress,
but strength to move on.
I love you,
but I gotta leave you alone.
Farewell.
So long...

II.

The Life Experience

P.O.E.T.R.Y.

I stand before you transparent and honest.
Thankfully and respectfully,
I share with you,
my poetry.
I give unto you,
confide in you,
take pride in giving this to you.
My words,
my thoughts.
My heart,
my soul.
Until I'm one hundred and one years old.
I live for this.
Die for this.
Listen to these words I spit.
This unexplainable feeling is something serious.
I love this and it returns the favor.
We made covenant something major.
A bond that could never be broken.
Spoken word is my passion.
My satisfaction.
No cheap thrills here because,
I gets mine.
Utilizing this gift that was given to me from the Divine.
My light will continually shine through each and every word that flows from my mouth.
P.O.E.T.R.Y.

Presenting **O**neself **E**nthusiastically **T**hrough **R**eleasing **Y**ourself.
That's why I do what I do.
Genuinely,
and with every fiber of my being.
Behind each piece is a meaning.
A picture painted.
A lesson learned,
or a moment shared.
For some, experiences that may have been too difficult to bear.
I say creativity at it's best.
If I could bless one person with words…mission accomplished.
Realize that poetry provides a knowledge and intelligence to those who did not know this existed.
Poetry built friendships with some of the truly gifted.
I've been blessed to find mine through this little light of mine.
This prize that dwell within me.
I've been blessed to inherit a spoken word family.
Acknowledge it because it lives and breathes life.
Embrace it for it's freedom.
Accept the stimulation it supplies for the mind.
Receive it for it's relevance.
Respect it for it's culture and abundance.
At the risk of being redundant,
I LOVE this, and it loves me.
I'm Erica Nicole,
signing out,
representing
P.O.E.T.R.Y.

A Haiku or Two

No one wants to die
Everyone wishes to live
What's reality?

Who knows true friendship?
Do tell the definition
What does Webster know?

Passionate kissing
Spirits connecting slowly
Here comes the soul tie

Will you marry me?
Not really sure who I be
I need a last name

Someone save me now
I don't know how to be free
Lend your angel wings

Unbelievable
In spite of all the drama
I'm still loving you

ColorMind

This fair skinned,
green eyed man,
held my hand after he opened the car door for me.
I felt like royalty.
A lady.
The Black Queen that I am,
the Black Queen that I am,
the Black Queen that I am.
A contradictory statement.
The crown on my cranium was removed by,
my hands,
with one glimpse of this man.
A confused mind,
questioning her own beauty.
Found comfort in those who reflected complexions of
smoke, tar, and chalk boards.
The Al B Sure's never appealed to her.
Vision Blurred.
Segregated mind state of her own race.
Case.
Not.
Closed.
Behold this beam of light
that took her off into the night,
displaying gentlemen-like tendencies.
Opened doors for me,

held out left hand for me,
something she never received.
Slavery embarked on the brain of
house and slave niggas,
feeling inferior to those who had decent residence.
Cooking and cleaning in Massah's domain,
While my black ass picked cotton in the field,
back being burnt by the hot, blazing sun.
Hooked on childhood memories of light-skinned
friend being prettier than me.
Suffered from ridicule in school of being left in the oven for too long.
Pain, hurt, and frustration never left.
Kept.
Stuffed into her memory bank,
gaining interest on every memory deposited,
to create a racist mind state.
Faced truth of prejudice.
Ashamed that I was the one to blame when it came to complexion preference.
Took a 2.5 journey to raise the lids of a beautiful kid who was unaware.
His face....bright.
Hair....blonde.
Eyes....green.
But failed to see that we share the same ancestry.
Was demanded to wake up without one word being spoken.
Optics opened.
Now seeing that I trapped myself into an
anti-positive way of thinking.
Blinking the dust out of my eyes to realize that no matter the color of my brothers,
I love you regardless.
Challenging was this process.

It took a male the opposite skin tone as me to see that we all are beautiful.
No race or complexion is better than the next.
We all are human beings with feelings and emotions just like the next.
Please believe that I've stepped out the box that kept me in rainbow bondage.
Healed,
renewed,
and delivered,
from the state of Colormind.

Kingship

(For every hard working man in the world, this is for you!)

You are royalty.
Majesty.
White collar.
Blue collar.
Academic scholar.
Entrepreneur, and everything under the sun connoisseur.
Fathers, Sons, Uncles, Brothers, Cousins and Husbands.
I honor you.
For everything you are and do.
Working 8 to 12 hour shifts just to get a whiff of the American Dream.
To live life successfully.
Set for life indubitably.
Striving, surviving, and providing for our families.
Head of Household.
King on the Throne.
Strong in mind,
Physically fine,
Holistically divine.
God fearing,
imaging Him.
Appreciated in every touch you give.

You are the reason we live, breathe,
and take heed in loving you so dearly.
So manly.
Forever willing to take a stand for me.
Taking aid in making sure all the bills are paid.
Never delayed when I need you.
One call away.
Dependable. Whole. Soulmate.
Escape from this cold and disrespectful world you face daily,
and let me cradle you in my bosom for I treasure you.
Dwell in this spirit where love reside.
Allow me to be your humble servant, and cater to you whole-heartedly.
Lay your burdens upon me, for I am Godly just like you.
Gracious man,
you are wonderful in every way imaginable.
Now I lay me down to sleep, I pray the Lord this man you'll keep.
Order his steps in all he does,
and let him know that he is admired, adorned, blessed, and loved...

This Face

Every since I was a child.
I never aspired to be America's Next Top Model.
Never been one to wear caked up Make-up.
My theory?
True beauty comes from within.
It's no sin to enhance what's already there,
but why not wear it bare?
It's not the painting of the exterior that makes up your make up.
I've replaced cosmetics with warm, natural earth tones of my own,
that connects with an untainted soul.
Maybelline and Cover-girl ain't got nothing on me.
See,
I apply astringent,
where I once laid foundation to conceal all the impurities that you used to see.
Where shimmery golds brushed across cheekbones reflect mountain tops high,
risen like the morning sun.
How can one hide the pureness in one's eyes by wearing tinted,
non-prescription contacts?
Ads for Mac mascara for longer eyelashes and eye shadows created in every color imaginable.
My lashes,
protect lens from dust as I blink.

Not bat for attention.
They cover chestnut brown pupils as I sleep, wish, think and dream for the embracing of my innermost being.
I receive it.
Cleave to it.
For it is me.
View the transparency of her bright eyes, white teeth, and warm smile that can light a tunnel for miles.
Appreciate the full lips that represent kin from way back when,
and elevated cheeks that makes her grin complete.
See me as the illustration of my Father.
No longer catering to what society says I should look like or be.
Let those smoothberry, creamkiss, and summerfruit shades exude from you.
Illuminating the totality of your own personality.
Do this for you,
as I do the same for me.
Look clearly into the mirror,
to a reflection that reads...
Priceless masterpiece.

Dreamed of My Father

She.
Slept a peaceful sleep.
Breathing easy and rhythmatic like the waves of the ocean.
Motion.
Slow.
Calm.
She fell into a place where she seen someone she haven't seen in years.
Her Father.
A tall man,
a sharply dressed man,
a thick grade of salt and peppered haired man.
Dreamed of my Father,
my Daddy,
my Papa.
Dreamed that he was there for me exclusively.
Dreamed that he cared for me righteously.
Envisioned little-bitty me,
a daddy's girl.
It felt so real, just wishing that it was real.
No longer wondered why my childhood friends Fathers lived with them,
and mine didn't.
No longer wondered why I couldn't call his house.

No longer wondered why the gifts that me and my brother bought him with my Mother's money was stuffed way in the back of his trunk.
No longer wondered why I have three sisters that I never met.
My Father.
The reason for my being.
Dreamed that I had the chance to meet his wife, and do the blended family thing.
Dreamed that he was there to see me off to prom.
Dreamed that he would be there to give me away at my wedding one day.
I dreamed this dream with a smirk on my face.
Hoping in my heart that this dream would never be replaced with the reality that arose when the lids of my eyes became ajar.
These words are not to bash him,
because my existence would be nothing if it was not for him.
Just left again hoping, wishing, praying that there was more than what I received.
Just emotionally greedy.
Hungry for the affection of a man that should have been originated from him.
My Father.
But instead I ran into the arms of my two brothers.
They spoiled me,
and aided me to be the Queen I stand to be.
Not Daddy.
I still love you because you partnered with my Mother in conceiving me.
Thank you.
But now I move on,
and put the past behind me.
You'll never be forgotten,

because we share the same memories.
They say I look like you.
While that may be very true,
I stand before you.
My own individual.
Strong, beautiful, free.

GOOD

This poetry,
is good.
Like never having to work again good.
Opening the door, seeing your soul mate and
marrying them good.
Living in your dream house,
driving your dream car,
never having to struggle again good.
Like Granny's Mac & Cheese and Collard Greens.
Winning the Mega Millions,
Norwegian Spring water good.
Touching a blue sky and kissing a rainbow,
satisfied on the inside,
humility to swallow your pride good.
Like staring in a full length mirror and loving your
naked body good.
Speaking words to encourage me;
once a month women never have to bleed again
good.
Like taking a bath in chocolate by Godiva,
sending your kids off to college without taking out
loans,
accomplishing all of your goals good.
Like recognizing your faults and becoming whole,
chicken soup for the soul,
having everything under control good.
Relaxed with no stress,

tender heart filled with love beating inside of my chest.
Like this is mine and you can't take it,
so glad we made it good.
Witnessing a child being born,
then a child being born again good.
Experiencing blessings flow like waterfalls from Mountaintops,
living and getting all of your dreams out good.
Like.....this poetry.

Empty

The single life is cool.
Having your own place,
your own space.
Freedom and independence is granted.
But...
What about the nights you lie in your
big, comfy, bed,
Alone?
I try to live,
single, saved, and satisfied.
But guess what?
It's hard, and temptation is strong.
Then ol' boy comes along asking....
Can I come through?
See,
I live by myself,
and I'm always by myself,
so I reply...
Yes.
We laugh, joke, and trip out.
Out of nowhere,
we begin to kiss,
touch, and such and such.
When it's over,
you leave,
and I'm left feeling...
empty.

Repeatedly,
week after week,
weekend after weekend.
You get yours,
but I never get mine.
Why does this continue to happen?
I'm sorry you asked.
Truth is,
there's an emptiness from within,
and when you're in me,
at that moment,
it's void.
When it's over, it returns.
My mind burns knowing that this is allowed due to,
self esteem issues and trues of un-fulfillment in
one's self.
How could one so strong be so weak?
I pray to God the Father to make me whole,
and give me the strength that I need to say no.
My prayer is interrupted my the ringing telephone.
It's him again.
Asking the same question.
I give him the same answer,
and perform the same act.
Wham Bam!
The door slams.
And again,
I'm empty.
So to my ladies and gents...
If you have a dude or chick,
you can call up and hit,
and have your way with.
I'm apologize but,
it's not necessarily because you're the "ish"....
They could just be..........Empty.

No Tears

(For Hubert C. Hyneman:
I'll always be your Nikki Giovanni)

Please.
Don't cry for me.
Instead,
smile for me.
I know that you'll mourn my absence with tears and sorrow,
but please rejoice in your soul for my home going.
Imagine a place where there is good news, praise, and daily worship.
Imagine a place of peace, joy, and comfort.
Where I now reside is more than what any human being could ask for.
There is no pain here,
No suffering,
No worries.
I've reunited with family members I thought I'd never see again.
I've witnessed the beauty of everlasting life.
Praise God for the gift of salvation and forgiveness, to dwell in this very place.
I'm home now, in the hands of Our Lord and Savior.
My purpose on earth has been carried out.

It's complete.
The same number of children I've been blessed to give life to.
Live out your purpose, for we're all just passing through.
Hold on to precious memories of me, as I'll do the same for you.
I love you, and I'll be watching over you.
Do not forget that Christ is with you.
He is a God of no mistakes.
Allow His comforting arms to hold you in this time of need,
and just know as I've entered the kingdom,
I've received my angel wings.
Don't fret dear child,
for this is not the end,
in His own time and place,
I'll see you again.
So please,
don't cry for me, I'm in a better place now....indeed.

The Definition: Poetry II

This is not a hobby.
This is pure,
unadulterated reality.
This is love, blood, sweat, and tears.
This is life,
This is dreams, goals, and aspirations.
This is therapy,
healing, mending, and feelings.
The pouring of the heart.
Pulsating, dripping,
red, black, or blue ink,
onto brown paper bags, recycled napkins, 3x5 post it notes, and windowed envelopes.
Stories of what shoulda, coulda, woulda happened, and still can.
This is man,
this is woman,
mother, brother, sister or cousin.
This loving one another.
Opening arms, thoughts, and emotions to perfect strangers.
Saying I know what you're going through,
without a one on one conversation.
This is the embracing of word play.
Metaphors, syllables, similes, and parenthesis.
I do not take this lightly.

It's freedom.
This cost nothing.
No price tags, or signs for sale, but a gift.
Given to me from my Father.
Something like the present.
Sowing seed to those in need.
It's the blood of Christ Lysol and Cloroxing me to disinfect all my iniquities.
It is nutrition for the mind of your body cause,
this is not a hobby.
This is pure, unadulterated reality.
It's come sit on the magic carpet Indian style storytelling.
This is enlightening.
Fighting.
Break ups to make ups, cause I love you, and there is no one else like you.
This is footprints in the sand.
The day that my Daddy carried me.
This is beauty, and all that it behold.
Bestowed upon I, or me.
We as poets have the ability to teach via spoken word,
hoping that it falls upon fertile ears.
This is not me,
it is He,
that allow these words to flow out of me.
This is fellowship.
This is learning, teaching, and growing one another.
This is family.
Extended, but still ready and willing to kill a rock over.
This is jazz,
this is the d'jembe, hip hop, r & b.

This is me.
This is desire,
spitting fire.
Only to burn the negativity that may be in the atmosphere.
This is caring,
sharing my life with you.
Maybe even a daydream or two.
This is soul searching,
finding your identity.
This is untitled pieces.
More like nameless children trying to find a way.
This is bare soles of feet slapping cold pavement, embracing the colors of this earth.
This is closing your eyes so that your hearing heightens.
This is Free.
This is Liberty.
Not those of Camouflage Finesse, but literally.
This is I cannot worry about what you think of me.
Cause this is not a hobby.
This is pure, unadulterated reality.
Some call it life,
I call it poetry.

A Haiku or Three or Four

We left each other
We both agreed upon this
I cried silent tears

Peace Joy Happiness
Causes me to stay humble
I will always praise

Cant fit my best jeans
I need to eat healthier
I'll start on Monday

I think of you now
And every once in awhile
I wish you were here

Hold me now dear love
This bond is so exclusive
Never let it fade

Chocolate brown eyes
Skin dark like a Hershey kiss
I imagine us

It's quite dangerous
To love anything too much
Please take much caution

SPEAK!

Call those things that be not,
as though they were.
I am a millionaire.
I want for nothing.
No longer do I struggle with finances,
and neither does my family.
Speak into your life as I speak into mine.
I am beautiful.
I am stress free.
I will get my degree.
I will own a home.
Or two, or three or four.
Hey,
maybe ten!
You can do it,
you can be it,
you can achieve it!
Do away with negativity,
and embrace the positive!
That's the way I'll live.
Forever and always,
til' the end of the days of my life.
A peace of mind is priceless.
So is good health.
I am so blessed,
to have had the opportunity to cross paths with
three living angels.
Mad Poet, Liberty, and L.S. Royal.

God showed me favor.
I walked into a place called the Kamikaze.
Vibe Session hosted by the folks of C.R.E.
Was shown love, support, and positivity.
Kudos to EACH AND EVERY ONE of you.
It's appreciated greatly.
Due to the wisdom and knowledge shared,
I am a better poet.
I speak it,
I shout it,
and let the whole world know it!
I speak great things into my life as well as others.
I'm a bad mutha......SHUT YO MOUTH!
But I won't.
I can't,
and I don't.
Do the evil that men do.
I will always and forever be true.
Not only to me,
but to you.
I will bless the Lord at all times.
His praise shall continually be in my mouth.
I was chosen to speak these words to you.
You,
you,
and you!
There is NOTHING in this world that you cannot do!
Who would have knew?
That the quiet, black girl with low self esteem,
and negative thinking would stand before you?
Changed.
No longer that girl.
She is gone.
Left behind.

I had to deal with the labor of renewing my mind.
Speak these things,
and again I say Speak!
These words go out to touch the meek,
and the bleak.
Hopefully one day you will learn something from me, and vice versa.
I used to think that I was cursed,
but I am not.
I am exceedingly and abundantly blessed.
I was made in the image of God.
Who can argue with that?
No one can disagree with facts.
Nor the truth.
Speak unto me,
as I speak unto you.
Speak life into the dying,
and speak comfort to the crying.
Let's unify and change the world.
Make our voices be heard.
SPEAK!